Oh, Bother! SOMEONE WON'T SHARE!

By Betty Birney
Illustrated by Nancy Stevenson

A GOLDEN BOOK • NEW YORK
Western Publishing Company, Inc., Racine, Wisconsin 53404

W9-BJB-798

"Fall is my favorite time of year," Rabbit thought as he worked in his garden one crispy cool morning. All around him the leaves had turned orange and gold, and the last of his vegetables were just about ready to be picked.

"It's my best crop yet," he thought.

In another part of the Hundred-Acre Wood, Winnie the Pooh was visiting his favorite honey tree. But the bees were not very happy to see him.

"*Bzzzz-bzzzz. Bzzzz-bzzzz,*" they hummed.

"What did you say?" asked Pooh.

"*Bzzzz-bzzzz-BZZZZZ!*" the bees answered, flying around Pooh's head.

Pooh raced away from the honey tree. When the bees stopped chasing him, Pooh stopped to catch his breath. But his tummy was feeling very rumbly.

"Oh, bother!" he said. "My honey jar is as empty as my tummy."

So Pooh decided to look for something else to eat.

Soon he reached Rabbit's garden. "Good morning,
Rabbit," said Pooh. "How is your garden today?"

"I have succulent spinach and luscious lettuce," bragged
Rabbit. "Over there are gorgeous green beans and colossal
carrots. Then there are my prized peppers and my
beautiful broccoli."

"Everything looks so tasty," said Pooh. "Do you think
you could share some of those carrots with me?"

"SHARE!" said Rabbit. "Why should I share?"
Pooh scratched his head and thought a bit. "Because
sharing makes you feel good," he replied. "And the more
you share with others, the more they'll share with you."

Rabbit could not believe his ears. "I worked hard to grow these vegetables," he told Pooh. "And I plan to eat them all winter. I can't give them away to anybody who happens to wander by!"

"Can't you?" asked Pooh, rubbing his empty tummy with his paw.

"No, I can't!" said Rabbit. "You should have planted a garden, the way I did."

As Pooh thought about planting a garden, he was interrupted.

"*Bzzzz-bzzzz-BZZZZZ!*"

The bees were back. This time Pooh ran after them, hoping he could get them to share their honey with him.

After Pooh left, Piglet visited Rabbit's garden.

"Good morning, Rabbit," said Piglet. "My, you have a lot of beautiful carrots."

"Yes, I do," replied Rabbit.

"Well . . . I have a little problem," Piglet explained. "I started to bake some carrot muffins, but I discovered that I didn't have enough carrots. If you will share a few of your carrots with me now, I will share my yummy carrot muffins with you later."

Rabbit shook his head and said, "Piglet, if I wanted carrot muffins, I would bake some myself. I'm sorry, but I won't share with you. Not today!"

Piglet left feeling very disappointed. "Rabbit is certainly not in a good mood," he thought.

Soon Tigger came bouncing into Rabbit's garden,
pushing Roo in a bright red wheelbarrow.

"Whee!" shouted Roo.

"Please stop bouncing! You'll bruise my broccoli!"
shouted Rabbit. "I suppose you want me to share some of
my vegetables with you."

"Nope," answered Tigger. "We came here to share the
wheelbarrow with you. It might help you harvest your
crop."

"Just bounce yourselves out of here before you crush my cucumbers," shouted Rabbit. "I don't want to share anything!"

As Rabbit chased Tigger and Roo away, he heard Tigger call, "Remember, Long Ears, the more you share with others, the more they'll share with you!"

"Nonsense," Rabbit muttered.

Later that day a wind howled across the Hundred-Acre Wood, blowing the dry leaves off the tree branches.

Suddenly the air was chilly, especially at Eeyore's Gloomy Place.

"Brrr! I believe the weather is growing brisk," said Owl, who was visiting. "It reminds me of when I was a wee owlet. There was an early frost that year, and the entire crop of vegetables was destroyed!"

"Even the thistles?" asked Eeyore.

"Even the thistles," Owl told him.

Eeyore thought of his friend Rabbit's garden and shook his head. "Uh-oh. I hope Rabbit's vegetables don't freeze."

"I think we should offer to help Rabbit," Owl suggested. Although Eeyore wasn't particularly pleased about going out in the cold, he agreed.

Soon Owl and Eeyore had gathered their friends together and told them that Rabbit's garden was in danger.

"If the vegetables aren't picked tonight, many could be ruined," Owl said.

"Oh, bother! What can we do?" asked Pooh. "Rabbit has worked so hard."

"Well, we can't change the weather," said Owl. "But we can help him harvest his crop quickly."

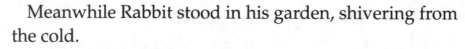

Meanwhile Rabbit stood in his garden, shivering from the cold.

"Oh, I'll never be able to pick all my beautiful vegetables before they freeze. All my hard work—for nothing!" he cried.

He didn't know that, at that very moment, his friends were busily gathering everything they needed to help him save his crop.

The friends arrived to find Rabbit frantically pulling carrots. "What are you doing here?" Rabbit asked them.

"You've worked hard on your garden," answered Pooh. "We want to help you save your vegetables."

Then Rabbit watched in amazement as Pooh shared his empty honey jars, placing them over the smallest lettuce plants to protect them from the cold so they could continue to grow.

Piglet shared his baskets to hold the vegetables as he and his friends quickly picked them.

Tigger and Roo shared their wheelbarrow to carry the vegetables to Rabbit's warm house. Owl's lanterns helped his friends see what they were doing, and Eeyore's blankets kept them warm.

All of Rabbit's friends shared their time and energy to help Rabbit harvest his vegetables and save them from the frost.

Hours later, after all the vegetables had been neatly piled in Rabbit's warm kitchen, the friends sat around the table, drinking hot chocolate. Rabbit felt so grateful to his friends that he said, "Thank you all for sharing with me. In return, I'd like to share my vegetables with you."

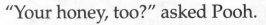

"Your honey, too?" asked Pooh.

"Well, uh . . . yes, I suppose so," Rabbit said with a sigh. He still wasn't *completely* used to sharing.

But when he saw how happy Pooh was to get the honey, Rabbit was glad he had agreed to share it.

"Are you sure you want to give us all these vegetables?"
Pooh asked Rabbit as they left.

"Sure, I'm sure," said Rabbit. "Sharing sort of grows
on you."

Tigger offered to share his wheelbarrow to help carry
the gifts home. And as the friends headed out into the
cold autumn night, they heard Rabbit call, "And just
remember what I always say: The more you share with
others, the more they'll share with you!"